For Una and Fiona, sisters forever

THIS IS A BORZOI BOOK PUBLISHED BY ALFRED A. KNOPF

Copyright © 2025 by Greg Pizzoli

All rights reserved. Published in the United States by Alfred A. Knopf,
an imprint of Random House Children's Books, a division of
Penguin Random House LLC, 1745 Broadway, New York, NY 10019.

Knopf, Borzoi Books, and the colophon are
registered trademarks of Penguin Random House LLC.

Visit us on the Web! rhcbooks.com

Educators and librarians, for a variety of teaching tools,
visit us at RHTeachersLibrarians.com

Library of Congress Cataloging-in-Publication Data is available upon request.
ISBN 978-0-593-64966-4 (trade) — ISBN 978-0-593-64967-1 (lib. bdg.) —
ISBN 978-0-593-64968-8 (ebook)

The text of this book is set in 17-point Sofia Pro.
The illustrations were created digitally.
Editor: Rotem Moscovich | Designer: Taline Boghosian | Copy Editor: Melinda Ackell
Managing Editor: Jake Eldred | Production Manager: Jen Jie Li

MANUFACTURED IN CHINA   10 9 8 7 6 5 4 3 2 1   First Edition

EARL & WORM
THE BAD IDEA
AND OTHER STORIES
GREG PIZZOLI

Alfred A. Knopf ✎ New York

Contents

Lemonade

Earl and Worm have been friends for a long, long time.

But when they first met, Worm was not so sure about Earl.

When Earl moved in next door,
Worm watched from her window.
"Who is that new bird?"
Worm said to herself.

"Why is he up so early?
And why is he smiling like that?
What is he so happy about?"

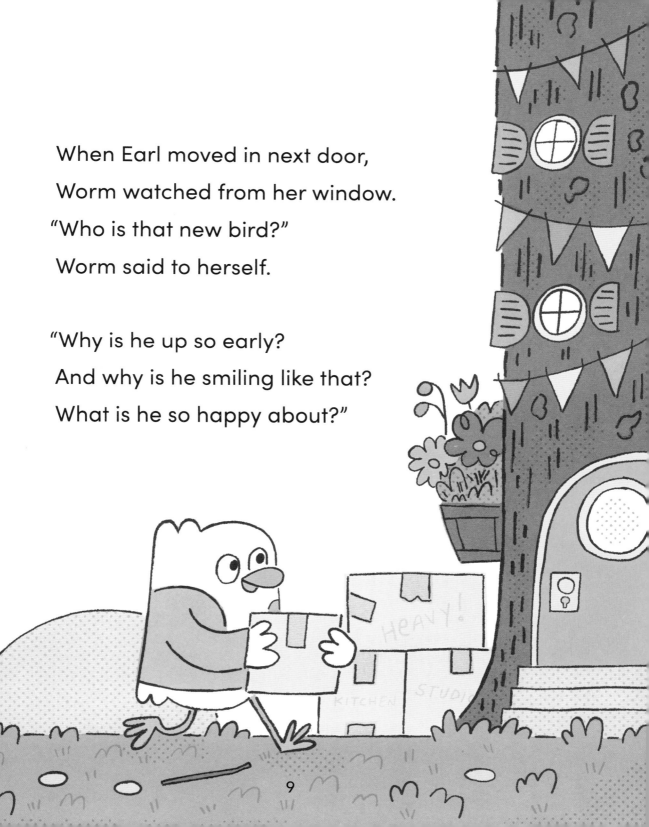

Earl saw Worm in the window.

"Hello! Yes, you there!

You must be Worm!

My name is Earl."

Earl waved.

He shouted, "Good morning!"

Worm ducked down out of sight.

She hid behind a book.

She did not say hello back.

"Good morning?" said Worm.

"What's so good about it?"

Worm was cranky.

She did not like new things.

And Earl was new.

A little while later,
Worm heard noises coming
from the garden next door.

"What is all that racket?"
said Worm.

She looked out her window.

Earl was playing music
in his garden.

Worm opened her window.
"Excuse me, Earl, can you
please be quiet?" said Worm.
"I am *trying* to read!"

"Oh, sorry, Worm!" said Earl.
"I was just playing music for my plants.
They love music in the mornings."

"Well, I do *not*!" said Worm,
and she slammed
her window shut.

13

The next day it rained.

Worm went to her kitchen

to make some tea.

On rainy days she liked tea

with milk and sugar.

There was a knock at the door.

It was Earl.

"Hello, Worm," said Earl.

"May I please borrow some sugar?"

"Oh, I don't know," said Worm.

"I don't have that much."

"Great! I don't need that much," said Earl.
He took the sugar and waved goodbye.

Worm sat down and drank her tea.

It was not sweet.

It was bitter.

So was Worm.

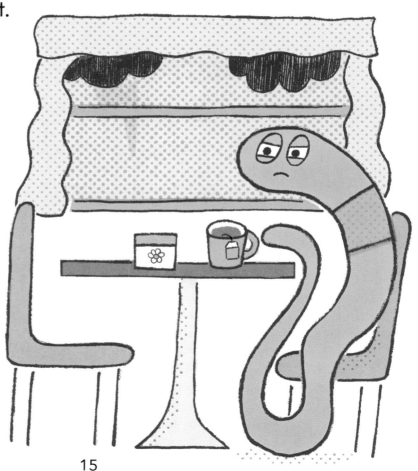

The next morning,
the sun shined in the sky.
Worm heard a noise outside.
"Worm! Are you there?"
It was Earl.
Not him again, thought Worm.

Worm came downstairs.
She opened her door.
"Good morning, Worm!" said Earl.
"I made some lemonade.
Would you like some?"

16

"I'm not thirsty," Worm grumbled.

Earl smiled.

"That's okay. We can just talk."

"I don't like to talk," said Worm.

"Perfect!" said Earl.

"I love to talk.

I can talk for both of us.

You can just listen."

Earl told Worm all about his life.

He talked about music.

He talked about his garden.

Worm just listened and

took a small sip of lemonade.

It tasted sweet.

Earl took a long drink.

He asked, "What about you, Worm?

What do you like?"

Worm was still grumpy.

She did not want to talk.

"I don't know," said Worm.

"I don't know what I like."

"Huh," said Earl.

"Okay, well, what *don't* you like?"

"I don't like people playing music
when I am trying to read!" said Worm.

Earl laughed.

"I'm sorry, Worm.

But my plants love music.

It helps them grow.

And isn't it nice to have

a garden out your window?"

Worm took a big
sip of lemonade.
"I guess. Yes. But I don't like
people taking all of my sugar!"
said Worm.

Earl laughed again.

"I'm sorry again, Worm.

But don't you like the lemonade?

I used your sugar to make it sweet."

Worm took a long sip.
It *was* very good lemonade.

"Do you know what
I don't like?" asked Earl.
"I don't like being alone."

Worm looked up at Earl.
"Oh," she said. "I don't like
being alone, too."

Earl smiled.

"Well, good," he said.

"At least that is one thing

we can agree on."

After a bit, Worm talked, too.
She told Earl about her life,
about her favorite books,
and about her favorite tea.

Worm invited Earl into her house.

Earl and Worm talked
for a long time.
Together they drank
all the lemonade.

They have been good friends ever since.

The Bad Idea

Worm was outside.

She was working in her garden.

Earl was outside, too.

Earl was working in his garden, too.

Worm stopped pulling weeds.

She looked up at her house.

"Huh," said Worm. "I just don't know."

Earl came over
to see what Worm
was looking at.

"What don't you know?"
asked Earl.

"I need to paint my
shutters," said Worm.
"But I don't know which
color to choose.
I am thinking maybe yellow."

"Yellow is a good color," said Earl.
"Yellow shutters sound very nice.
That sounds like a good idea."

"Okay!" said Worm.
"I will go with yellow.
Thanks, Earl!"

The next morning,
Worm woke up early
to paint her shutters.

When she went outside,
Earl was outside, too.
He was on a ladder.
He was painting his shutters.
He was painting them yellow.

"Earl, what are you doing?"
asked Worm.

"I am painting my shutters yellow,"
said Earl.

"But you copied me!"
said Worm. "That was MY idea!"

Earl shrugged.
"But I like yellow, too, Worm.
And a good idea is a good idea."

"Yeah. Real good idea, Earl,"
grumbled Worm.

Worm painted her
shutters yellow, too.
They looked a lot like
Earl's shutters.

"Great shutters!" said Earl.
"They look really good."

"Um, thanks," said Worm.
"But now I have another idea.
I am going to paint
my flower box blue."

"Really?" asked Earl. "I like blue.
A blue flower box is a good idea."

"It is MY good idea," said Worm.

"Yes, it is YOUR good idea," said Earl.

Worm painted her flower box blue.

She painted and painted for a long time.

"Finally! I am done," she said.

"Wow! That looks great!" said Earl.

"It looks just like mine."

"Huh?" said Worm.

It was true.

Earl had painted his flower box, too.

He had painted it blue.

"But that was MY IDEA!" said Worm.

"You *stole* my idea!"

"Sorry, Worm," said Earl.

"But I like blue.

And a good idea is a good idea."

39

"You copied me again!" said Worm.

She was angry.

She went inside her house.

She slammed the door.

She paced around the room.

Then she got an idea.

A *sneaky* idea.

A *tricky* idea.

A sneaky, tricky way to get back at Earl.

She went back outside.

She looked up at her house.

She smiled a sneaky smile.

Then, in a very,

very loud voice, she said,

"What a great idea!"

Earl came over quickly.

"What is a great idea, Worm?"

"Oh, *hello,* Earl," she said.

"I just had a great idea.
Tomorrow, I am going to
paint my whole house.
I am going to paint it orange,
with green stripes
and purple polka dots.
The whole house!
Isn't that a great idea?!"

"Huh," said Earl.
"Are you sure that
is a good idea?"

"It is a GREAT idea,"
said Worm.

Worm was being
very, *very* sneaky.

She said to herself:

"Earl will copy
my idea again.
He will paint his house
ALL of those UGLY colors!

Then he will learn
his lesson,
and he will STOP
copying me!"

The next morning, Worm got up early.

She could not wait to see Earl's house.

She went outside, and there was Earl.
He had his ladder and his paintbrush.

Worm smiled a sneaky smile.
"Good morning, Earl," she said.
"Are you going to do some painting?"

"I just finished," said Earl.
"I am sorry I copied you before.
I hope painting your house makes up for it."

Worm turned around.
She looked at her house.
It was orange.
Orange with green stripes
and purple polka dots.

It
was
very,
very
ugly.

"You know, Worm," said Earl.
"I was not so sure
about this idea.
But I have to say,
I kind of like it now."

50

Worm gulped.

"Um . . . thank you, Earl."

"You are so welcome," said Earl.

"See you later, Worm!"

Worm was alone
outside of her house.
She hated the way
it looked.

She sighed
a long,
deep
sigh.

"Well, Worm," she said to herself,
"a bad idea is a bad idea."

She went inside
to get her paintbrush.

The Poem

Worm was at her writing desk.

She was writing a poem.

It was not going well.

Roses are red,

Violets are blue,

Apples are sweet,

And so are . . .

"Hmmm," said Worm.

"Apples are sweet,

and so are . . . *what?*"

She went to ask Earl for help.

She knocked on Earl's door.

Earl smiled when he saw Worm.

"Hello, Worm," he said.

"How are you?"

"I am not good at all!" said Worm.

"I am trying to write a poem.

But I do not know how to finish it."

"Read it to me," said Earl.

"I will help you finish it."

So Worm read
her poem to Earl.

"*Roses are red,*
Violets are blue,
Apples are sweet,
And so are . . ."

"This is a good poem," said Earl.
"A good start."

"Thank you," said Worm.

"But what you really need,"
said Earl, "is a good ending."

"I know! I agree!" said Worm.
"Can you help me?"

"Of course!" said Earl.
"Come inside. I am sure we
can finish this poem together."

"How about . . .

Roses are red,
Violets are blue,
Apples are sweet,
And so are lemons."

59

"What?" said Worm.
"No, Earl, that will not work."

"Why not?" asked Earl.

"Well, it does not make sense,"
said Worm. "Lemons are not sweet.
Lemons are sour."

"That's true," said Earl.

"And it does not rhyme," said Worm.
"The ending should rhyme
 with the word *blue*."

"Oh, okay," said Earl.
"Well, how about this?"

"Roses are red,
Violets are blue,
Apples are sweet,
And so is Lou."

"Lou? Who is Lou?" asked Worm.

"Lou is my cousin," said Earl.
"He is very sweet."

"I DO NOT KNOW LOU!" cried Worm.

"You would like him," said Earl.

"This is not helping me, Earl!"
yelled Worm. "I am going home!"

Worm got home
and sat down
at her writing desk.
She thought and
she thought and
she thought.

After a few minutes,
Worm went from being mad
to feeling kind of bad.

She felt bad for yelling at Earl
because Earl was only trying to help.

Earl is a good friend, thought Worm.

"That's it!" cried Worm.
She wrote and she wrote,
and she finished her poem.

Worm rushed outside to find Earl.

"Earl!" cried Worm. "I am sorry!
You were right about my poem.
It does not need to make sense.
It does not need to rhyme."

"I think you are right," said Earl.
"But what does a poem need to do?"

"It needs to tell the truth,"
said Worm.
"I finished my poem.
Can I read it to you?"

"Of course," said Earl.

Earl sat down on a rock
and listened to Worm
read her poem.

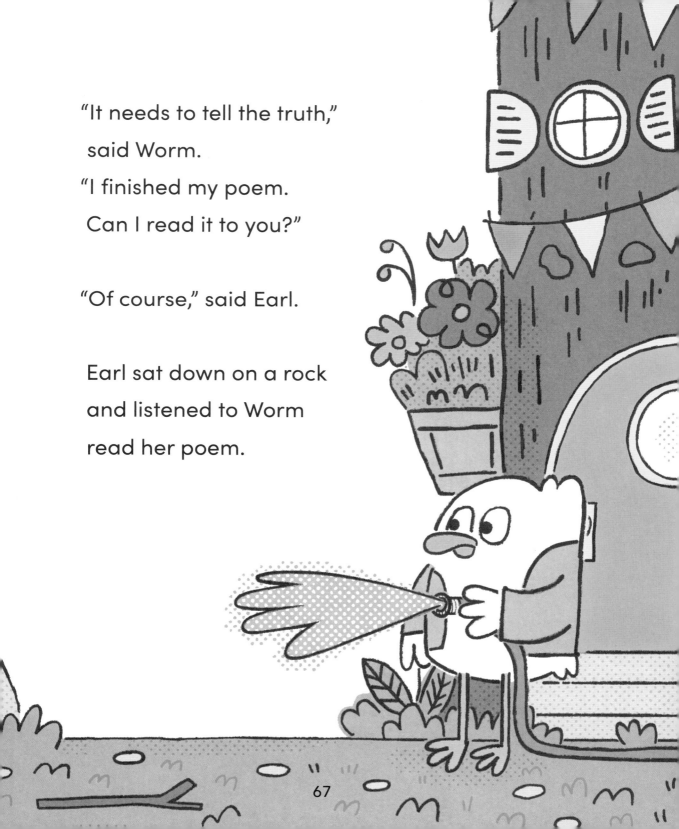

"Roses are red,
Violets are blue,
Apples are sweet,
and Earl is my best buddy."

"It is perfect!" said Earl.
"It tells the truth."

"Thank you," said Worm.

"Read it again," said Earl.

And they sat on the rock together,
and read the poem again

and again

and again.

The End